The Rat-Catcher of Hamelin

Written by June Crebbin

Illustrated by Caroline Romanet

Collins

Chapter 1

On the banks of a great river in northern Germany, there is a town called Hamelin.

Once, many years ago, the townsfolk of Hamelin lived happy and contented lives. They worked hard. Their crops grew. Their harvests were plentiful.

The bakeries were full of newly baked loaves. The butchers sold tasty cuts of meat. The gardeners grew all manner of fruit and vegetables. The people helped each other. They made good laws. They kept the peace. But one day, that peace was broken.

Rats!

Of course, there'd always been rats in Hamelin,
scuttling after the grain in the storehouses, but
the town cats had soon got rid of those. Now, rats
swarmed through the town – hundreds of them, fierce
and mean and hungry.

They ate the grain in the storehouses. They ate the cheeses in the dairies. They ate the meat hanging on hooks in the pantries. They tumbled into barrels and drank until they were full. They streamed into shops and houses, attacking anyone in their path. Mothers snatched up babies out of their cots and held them close.

Older children tried to run out of the way, but the rats were quicker with their mean little eyes and their sharp, pointy teeth. They bit deep and scratched deeper. Within hours, where the skin was broken, ugly red patches appeared, blisters and swellings. Children cried out in pain and many lay sick with fever, struggling to breathe.

The townsfolk locked their doors and kept
the windows tightly shut, even though the air was
thick with the summer heat. At night, no one could
sleep, listening to rats scrabbling and chewing
under floorboards. But they dreaded daylight more,
when they could see them, and they knew disease
from the rats would spread. Rats were everywhere,
in every street and alley.

Nothing and no one was safe.

"Something has to be done, and done quickly," said one citizen. So the townsfolk met in the marketplace.

"What can we do?" said another citizen.

"Set the cats on them!" someone cried. "That's what we usually do." But by then, the cats were either dead or too scared.

"We must put down traps," said another. So traps were set all over the town. But the rats, clever rats, weren't tempted by the food in the traps. They knew how to chew their way into sacks of grain. They knew how to squeeze through the tiniest holes into shops and houses. They knew where to find plenty of food.

9

"We must put down poison," said another.
"That'll finish them." But the rats, clever rats, took one sniff and left it alone.

"Get rid of their nests!" cried another citizen.
So the people of Hamelin went out with pikes
and sticks and poked out the nests and blocked up
the holes. But the rats, clever rats, made new nests in
different holes.

Days passed, and still the rats swarmed through the town. Food began to run out. Shops were closing because there was nothing to sell. Worst of all, disease carried by the rats was spreading. The townsfolk knew it could cause death.

"We must go to the mayor!" someone said at last. "He's a clever man. He'll be able to help us."

So the townsfolk left their houses and their shops and marched along the streets to the town hall.

"The mayor will know what to do," they said to each other.

12

But the mayor didn't know what to do. For days he'd been thinking and thinking.

Chapter 2

From his window in the mayor's office at the town hall, he'd seen the townsfolk rushing to and fro. He'd seen them setting traps, putting down poison and poking out nests.

But nothing had stopped the rats.

The mayor had no idea what to do. But he knew the townsfolk would come to him. If there'd ever been any problems in the past, he'd been the one they consulted. They relied on him.

He sat in his office, alone, his head sunk in his hands. Suddenly, there was a loud rapping at the huge oak door.

The mayor pulled his fur cloak more tightly around his shoulders. He adjusted his gleaming gold chain of office. He opened the heavy door. A storm of voices greeted him.

"We need your help!"

"Our children are sick from rat bites. Our animals are sick and dying."

"What can we do?"

"Tell us what to do."

The mayor held up his hand. He drew himself up.
The crowd quietened. "First," he said, "there's no need
to worry – "

There was an instant outcry. "Worry?" someone shouted.
"Wouldn't you worry if your child was lying ill with
a fever, close to death?" Other angry voices joined in.

"Don't you know we're near to starving?"

"Don't you know we've tried everything we can think of to get rid of the rats?"

Again, the mayor held up his hand. But this time, the crowd didn't quieten.

"No use hiding in there!" a voice cried. "What are you going to do?"

And the loudest voice of all shouted, "What do you think we pay you for?"

The mayor held up his hand once more. He tried to keep it from shaking. He thought quickly. "I call upon the councillors," he said. The councillors came forward in twos and threes through the restless crowd.

The heavy door shut behind them as they entered the town hall. They took their places round the huge oak table in the mayor's office.

"Think!" instructed the mayor. "Think. Our lives depend on it."

For two hours the councillors sat. No one spoke. No one moved. No one could think of anything.

Outside, the crowd could be heard mumbling. The mumbling grew to a grumbling. The grumbling grew to a rumbling.

Suddenly, there was a tap, tap,
tapping at the town hall door.
The mayor started up in his chair.
But, if he opened the door,
the crowd might surge in. He kept
his seat. The tap, tap, tapping
came again.

"Who is it?" called the mayor.

The door swung open, easily, as if
it had just been oiled. In stepped
the strangest figure you've ever
seen – a tall thin man, dressed
half in yellow and half in red,
and on his head, was a hat with
a feather. Around his neck, on
a silver chain, hung a silver pipe.
Behind him, the crowd had
fallen silent, watchful.

The stranger spoke. "I can rid your town of rats,"
he said.

The mayor sat up. He couldn't believe his luck.
Just when he thought all was lost, this stranger had
come to save him. It was a miracle.

"I've rid towns of toads and newts," continued
the stranger. "I've rid towns of beetles and bats. If you
pay me a thousand gilders, I'll rid your town of rats."

The mayor leapt to his feet. "A thousand?" he cried. "If you can rid our town of rats, we'll give you 50,000!"

The councillors leapt to their feet. "Agreed!" they cried. "Agreed!"

Outside, the offer was repeated from one citizen to another. A burst of clapping and cheering broke out.

"Tomorrow," promised the stranger, "there won't be a rat left in Hamelin."

Away went the townsfolk to their homes, marvelling at the man who was going to give them back their town.

"How will he do it?" the mayor's son asked his father that night at bedtime.

The mayor smiled. He was thankful his only child had so far not been bitten by a rat. "Tomorrow we'll know," he said. Tomorrow his son would be safe.

Chapter 3

The following day, at dawn, the sound of a pipe drifted into Hamelin town. Through the streets stepped the piper, playing a strange and lilting tune. It seemed to flow through the very walls of the quiet houses. It reached into the furthest corners and up to the rafters. It wrapped itself round every room.

Out flocked the rats, from attics and cellars, from gables and gutters, from under floorboards and out of cupboards. Out they tumbled from every nook and cranny, every street and alley. There were hundreds of rats, of every size and colour: lean rats, fat rats, brown rats, black rats, all falling over themselves in their haste to follow the piper.

28

After them hurried the townsfolk, watching and wondering, marvelling and muttering. Where was the piper going?

Up and down, in and out of the squares and alleys, the piper strode, collecting rats at every turn, until you could barely see the cobblestones there were so many, and such a squeaking and a squealing as the town had never heard before.

Then the piper turned
away from the town.
Down he marched to
the river and, though he
stopped at the water's
edge, the tune went on.

The rats went on. Into the river they streamed until not a single rat was left on the bank.

And every one was drowned. The townsfolk went wild with joy. They cheered and clapped the piper as he made his way through the crowds to the mayor.

"A thousand gilders, if you please," he said. "As we agreed."

The mayor went pale. A thousand gilders? A thousand gilders would pay for a good many council dinners.

"Never," he said to the piper. "Be off with you. We saw the rats drown in the river with our own eyes. I don't think they're going to bother us again."

The piper flushed in anger, but he spoke quietly. "You'll regret a broken promise," he said.

The councillors muttered among themselves.
"Maybe we should –"

"No need!" cried the mayor. "Think of it. We've saved
ourselves a thousand gilders." He turned to the crowd.
"A thousand gilders will build you new houses,
provide you with new wagons and carts, and pay to
clean up the damage caused by the rats."

There was a pause. Then a voice shouted,
"The mayor's right. The piper shouldn't need paying."
Other voices joined in, shouting their agreement.
All eyes turned on the piper.

"A promise should be kept," he said, as he
walked away.

Chapter 4

That night, the townsfolk of Hamelin slept soundly in their beds, knowing the rats had gone.

Towards dawn, the first notes of a strange and lilting tune drifted through the streets of Hamelin. Only the children heard.

One by one, they rose from their beds. Out they flocked from their houses, laughing and chattering, skipping and dancing, little ones and big ones, all drawn by the magic of the piper's tune, all following after.

But the parents and the grandparents, aunts and uncles didn't stir. They lay, warm and cosy in their beds, in a deep, deep sleep.

The mayor's son rose from his bed and looked out of his window. He saw the piper and the children following. He heard the piper's tune. Out he danced to join them. The line of children grew longer and longer.

Up and down, in and out of the squares and alleys, the piper strode, collecting children at every turn, until you could barely see the cobblestones. There were so many, and such a happy singing and chattering as was never heard before.

Then the piper led the children away from the town. Down he marched to the river. But there, he turned aside and led the long procession through meadows wild with summer flowers. He led them through woods alive with birdsong. He led them over the stone bridge across the river. He took them through a dark forest and out into the sunlight.

Up a steep and rocky path
they climbed until they
came to a huge mountain.
It blocked their path.
But the piper didn't stop.
He led them on and, as
they reached the foot
of the mountain,
there was a
great cracking
and grinding.

The mountain split open right in front of them. Beyond was a cave. In strode the piper. In danced the children and, when the last child had been swallowed up into the darkness, the mighty rock closed so that you couldn't see where the split had been.

Only one child was left outside.
A boy who'd hurt his leg
hadn't been able to keep up
with the others, and had
arrived too late. But he'd
caught a glimpse of
the land which lay
beyond the cave.
Slowly, sadly, he
made his way back
to the town.

Meanwhile, the townsfolk had woken up and were
searching desperately for their children. They met
the boy at the river's edge. He tried to comfort them.
He told them of the beauty which lay beyond the cave.
He told them how the children had followed the piper,
laughing and singing. "They were happy," he said.

But the townsfolk were overcome with sadness.
They journeyed to the mountain that day, and many
days after, searching and searching for their
lost children.

Hamelin town lies on the banks of a great river in
northern Germany.

There, and all over the world, from that time to this, the story of the rat-catcher has been told. It's the story of a broken promise, of a piper with magic in his tune and of a mountain that never gave up its secret.

Who lives in Hamelin?

before the piper

the first time
the piper plays

the last time
the piper plays

47

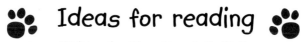

Ideas for reading

Written by Clare Dowdall, PhD
Lecturer and Primary Literacy Consultant

Reading objectives:
- ask questions to improve understanding
- make predictions from details stated and applied
- identify main ideas drawn from more than one paragraph and summarise ideas

Spoken language objectives:
- participate in discussions, presentations, performances, role play, improvisations and debates

Curriculum links: PSHE – health and wellbeing

Resources: whiteboard and pens; paper plates; string and paint for mask making; music for rat dance; ICT for research

Build a context for reading

- Ask children what they think about rats. Create a pets and pests chart to record some positive and negative ideas about them.
- Look at the front cover and read the title. Ask if any children know this story and to share what they know.
- Read the blurb together. Discuss whether you should trust strange mysterious people if they offer to help you.

Understand and apply reading strategies

- Read aloud to p5. Ask children to listen for the problem that's being described and to recount it.
- Challenge children to read with a partner to the end of Chapter 1, looking for language that describes the rats.
- Discuss some examples of descriptive language, and ask children to describe how it makes them feel about the rats.